Two Family Fables of Christmas

Written, Published and Illustrated
by- Michael Schall Johnson
edited by- Madeline Johnson

2020 First Edition
Johnson Publishing
and Design Company
Summerlin, Las Vegas, Nevada
© 2020

On the Trail of a Christmas Pony

Little Ruth went to watch Papa and Grandpa, as she always did on Saturday mornings when she had no school. The blacksmith shop was an interesting place for little Ruth. Grandpa was an old school blacksmith who enjoyed making his own nails and horseshoes. They always had time for this curious little eleven year old, even when they were very busy. She loved to hear the old stories about the war that Grandpa was in. She was quite impressed with the story about how he shod the General Grant's horse, but she was sorta tired of it.

She said, "Tell me a fun story, not about the war that Grandpa Floyd was in and it was great when he crossed the Missouri in 1871 with two spans of mules, I love that one, but I've got it memorized!"

"Well hon, when you get old, you'll learn that the triumphs of your youth might be the only thing you have left.....okay now...Once there was a young Princess...."

She put her hand over her dad's mouth and stopped him, "I've heard Princess's stories until I'm kinda tired of them."

"Well, what kind of story shall I tell, then?"

"How 'bout Christmas. It's getting awful close. Maybe about a girl that gets a pony for Christmas."

"It seems to me, that you might have a sneaky purpose to want a story like that," her papa said, "I've told you more tales about pony's than I have about Princess's."

"Ponies are more interesting."

"Well!" Her papa roused himself from his shoeing job and handed her the large horse's tether. "Okay, just hold on to this big guy for me and I'll tell you about a little girl that wanted a pony every Christmas. How would you like that?"

"First-rate!" said little Ruth; and she held on to the tether of the great horse, ready for listening.

"Very well then, once upon a time there was a Prince....Oh, why are you pounding me?"

"Because you said Prince and not a little girl."

"I should like to know what's the difference between a little girl and a Prince?"

"Papa," said Little Ruth, playfully, "if you don't tell me about the pony, I won't listen to more of yer ol war stories!"

He loved to tease little Ruth, but he knew he was defeated so began the story. She wanted.

"Well, once there was a little girl who liked ponies and she wanted one in the worst way for Christmas every year. So as soon as Thanksgiving was over, she began sending postcards to Santa asking if she might have a pony. But old Saint Nick never answered any of her postcards; and

finally someone told her that Santa was a little picky and only noticed letters on sheets of paper in sealed envelopes. So, then, she sent a letter in an envelope; and in about three weeks, just the day before Christmas.... she got an answer from Santa, saying she might have a Christmas a pony if she was good every day for a year and then he would see about fitting one into his sleigh. The little girl was excited about his letter. As she prepared for the old-fashioned, once-a-year Christmas that was coming the next day. Perhaps with what Santa had written, she wouldn't have to wait a whole year to make such an impression on him as she would have at some other time. She was resolved to keep the letter to herself and surprise everybody with it, if it came true; and then she erased the pony from her mind altogether."

"The family had a splendid Christmas Eve decorating, the little girl helped with the big Christmas-tree, they had it lighted and standing in the middle of the living room. She went to bed early, so as to let Santa Claus have a chance to come. In the morning she was the first one up of anyone and found her stocking all lumpy with packages of candy, oranges, grapes and a small present. Her brothers and sisters, all with the same and her eldest sister with a new silk umbrella. Her papa's and mamma's stockings were filled with oranges and grapefruit wrapped up in tissue-paper, just as they always received every Christmas. Then she waited around till the rest of the family were up, they all had a splendid Christmas day. She ate so much candy that she a stomach ache; and the whole day the presents kept pouring in and she went around the family giving out the little presents she had made them. She went outside and looked for a larger present in the stable. All she found was a note from Santa, 'Dear little girl, sorry no pony this year due to the acute shortage of hay in Nebraska.' Then she went back into the house with her stomach-ache, crying; and her papa told her, 'A hay-burner is all a pony is good for.' She couldn't even eat the

turkey and cranberries for dinner nor the plum pudding with nuts and raisins. She peeled an orange and nibbled on it. Later the family had a light supper and everybody went to bed early in a bad mood."

Little Ruth patted her papa in the back, again and frowned.

"What now? Did I say Prince?"

"Now, you jist told me a sad Christmas story!"

"Well, wasn't she sad?

"No matter; you oughtn't tell a story like that to a little girl like me, especially for Christmas!"

"Very well, then, I take it all back."

Ruth decided, as it was November, it was time to write a letter to Santa and this was going to be the best letter she knew how to write.

"Dear Santa, I am writing to thank you for all the great presents you have given me in the past, so I don't really need anything. Just bring my sisters and brothers the things they want. I will see to it that there is some of Mama's fresh chocolate chip cookies, with walnuts, the way that Mama says you like them, along with some fresh milk from our cow. And by the way you might keep an eye out for a pony, if you just happen to run across one, I might like. Hopefully it would fit in your sleigh. I don't mind if you can't swing it, but I thought I would mention it, just in case. I am a good girl and help my pop and grandpa in the blacksmith shop. I don't fuss with my brothers and sisters too much. Love Ruth Cornwell, Walthill, Nebraska."

Saturday mornings bright and fresh came and went at the Cornwell farm and brimming with life. There was a song in every heart; the music issued at the lips. There was cheer in faces and a spring in every step. The sycamore trees had turned gold and were losing their leaves and the fragrance of autumn filled the air. The farm's green was gone, and the vegetation was ready for winter, a delectable farm, dreamy, restful, and inviting.

Ruth had made it for eleven years without a pony, so surely, she could go on another year without one. Yet today, as she gazed at the wintry countryside, she became conscious that something might happen. It was Christmas next week. She smiled at the thought. Then she noticed the figure of Papa coming up the road. He came in the front door.

"Ruth!"

She went slowly in answer to the summons. He held a letter in his hand.

"Met the postman," he said, "it's from Santa."

She opened the letter and read it;

"Dear Ruth , thank you for your sweet letter, I know you are a nice little girl. I have my best Elf working on finding you a pony, as you might understand, they are scarce up here. You have a nice family and I always try to do my best for nice people, love to you all, Santa."

Ruth said nothing. She liked to talk with her papa. But she was disappointed and at a loss for words.

"All right," Papa said at last, in an answer to her silence, "what'd he say?"

"He said maybe."

"Well that's pretty good!"

Papa went with three of Ruth's brothers in their big sleigh, that Grandpa Floyd had built, to cut a tree. They waited until Christmas Eve to put it up, the tree was lit by candles, so it wasn't safe to keep one up longer than a day or two. It was decorated with items that were all made by family members; wreaths, garlands, lights, candles, goodies, toys, stockings, ribbons, bows and nutcrackers. Mama and Grandma baked cookies, cakes and pies.

"Let's all pile in our brand new touring car and go to Walthill and see all the grand Christmas decorations!" said Papa, he hoped this would cheer up little Ruth.

This brought delight to everyone but Gramps and Gram who had decided to retire early and declined.

So, eleven kids, two adults all jumped in the big blue touring car. The scene in Walthill was white crystal in shop windows, lights gleaming on the slippery streets, mobs of last-minute shoppers and posters cheerfully advising people to do their shopping early. In front of the drug store. There was a tall Santa Claus, bearded and red-cheeked, with a scarlet-coated, white-furred and garland of holly on his cap. On street corners, there were elves ringing Salvation Army bells and brightly colored Christmas magazines on the newsstand. There were wreaths for sale at the flower stand and a peddler on the corner selling glossy holly from a crate. The town was bustling with activity on this Christmas eve.

The kids all went to bed early and excitedly, finally it was Christmas Eve. Little Ruth slept very heavily that night dreaming about ponies and she slept a little late, she was awoken at last by her sisters and brothers "What is it?"

said Ruth, and she rubbed her eyes and tried to rise up in bed.

"Christmas! Christmas! Christmas!" They all shouted and waved their stockings.

"Christmas morning!"

Her brothers and sisters just laughed. "We know that it's Christmas today, come into the living room and see."

She was dreadfully sleepy, but she sprang up and darted into the living room. Then all at once it dawned on little Ruth that Santa might be keeping his promise, everyone had such nice presents and her pony might be here, but she didn't see it.

"Papa, where is my pony?"

He took her around the tree and then he pointed out all the great things Santa had left, but, alas, no pony in sight. "You needn't go over it all again, papa; I guess I can remember what is here," said little Ruth.

The whole family surrounded the Christmas tree unwrapping their presents, but looking pretty sleepy. Her father sat with his arm around Mama, who was ready to cry. "Isn't this the best Christmas ever, Ruth?" She asked.

Her father said, "It seems I might be dreaming I thought I smelled a pony. This struck little Ruth as not the best kind of a joke; and she had eaten too much nuts and candy, she didn't want any breakfast, she went outside, first to the barn and then to the blacksmith shop. She was reluctant to ask her papa to help look for the pony, he might think her ungrateful and a little bratty. But she could hardly stand it. She was sure she could bear it if there was no pony. So, she went back in the house, resolved to the fact that there was really no pony and maybe she would put her mind on her other presents.

"Papa!"

"Well, what now?"

"Did Santa forget his promise?"

"Oh! He didn't exactly promise, did you look outside?"

His tone brought new hope to Ruth and she began to get excited. "Yes, I did!"

Then Papa said, "Come on let's go have another look," as he took little Ruth by the hand.

As they walked outside, Papa asked, "Did you look in the orchard pasture?"

"No, let's take a look!" she could hardly contain herself now.

It was a brisk winter day; they saw a bucking pony kicking up her heels. "Oh, Papa she is so spirited, do you think we can we catch her?"

"Your horse is frisky because it's cold out! But how did you know she was a mare?"

"I just knew! She is so beautiful, let's call her Crazylegs. Is she all mine ?"

"That's what you wanted Santa to bring you, he came through for you."

They tried to catch Crazylegs in the orchard pasture, they found this pony entirely too playful to catch. In response to Papa's whistling she came galloping toward them. But when Crazylegs caught sight of the rope that Papa held in his hand, she stopped short. And she snorted, as if to say, "I don't believe I'll go with you. I'm having too much fun."

So Ruth walked toward her and waited until her new young master reached out a hand to take hold of her mane and Crazylegs wheeled like a flash and tore off across the pasture, leaving Ruth grabbing at the empty air.

Ruth chased her, crying, "Whoa! Whoa!" It seemed that the faster Ruth ran after her the faster the pony went. So, Ruth soon fell into a walk. At last Crazylegs stopped and waited for her, pricking up her ears at Papa's whistle.

"This is great sport!" Papa chuckled as she dashed away again.

Ruth, however, did not think it sporting After following Crazylegs all over the pasture she was worn out.

Back toward the gate, she turned at last and climbed over the fence, she looked at Crazylegs, who stood on a knoll regarding her pleasantly.

"I'll get you yet!" Ruth called. "You needn't think you can beat me!"

"What shall I do?" Ruth asked Papa. "I can't catch Crazylegs. I've been trying for a half hour. And she won't let me get near enough to grab her."

Papa laughed, "I was just letting you have a little fun getting acquainted. She is a tease," he said. "You'll have to coax her with oats. Put a few handfuls of oats in a bucket and hold it up so she can see it. Shake it, too, she'll hear those oats swishing around, that'll get her!"

Ruth was quick to carry out her father's plan. And she was smiling as she stepped through the gate, holding the bucket and shaking it to hear the rustling of the oats.

Then her father called to her. "You'd better keep that rope behind you, when you get to the pasture, if Crazylegs sees it she might not come...oats or no oats."

Ruth giggled as she clutched the rope carefully behind her back and the bucket of oats in the other. She walked slowly toward the pony. Papa helped her with short, sharp whistles. Crazylegs soon came cantering up from the other side of the pasture, as she neared Ruth she slowed down to a walk.

Ruth stood still and shook the oats, holding it up so that Crazylegs could see it, she whinnied. The pony knew that sound. She knew it was the best thing to eat on the farm. She moved forward a few steps, stopped, sniffed and at last came straight up to Ruth and thrust her nose into the grain measure. While she was munching the oats little Ruth passed the rope loop around her neck.

"There, I've got you!" Ruth cried.

Papa said, "Put the loop on top of her head, behind the ears and over her snout. Then you make a little twist under her mouth and pass the rope through it and there you have it, a halter."

Crazylegs acted as mild as milk toast. She stood still while Ruth made the halter as Papa guided her, "And now, young lady, you'll never lead me on such a merry chase again," said Ruth. Then she followed Ruth to the pasture, down the lane, and into the barn. "I got her, why didn't we try the oats right off?"

Papa said. "I thought this would be more fun for you to get to know her a little, ponies like oats better than anything."

Two Family Fables of Christmas

Little Ruth said, "Thank you Papa this is the greatest Christmas ever." And then she put her arms around him and kissed him. She said, "A Christmas like this will never, never come again!"

Papa frowned and asked her, "You should thank Santa."

Little Ruth asked herself, why not? This made her think it all over carefully. The best Christmas in a hundred years, Santa had pleased people ever since Christmas began. She said, "I will write Santa and tell him my Christmas was first rate!"

"He probably already knows, but that would be nice, let's have some dinner," said Papa.

She was really not hungry and was a little reluctant about leaving her pony so soon.

Her mama put her head out the door and yelled, "Are you two never coming to dinner? What have you been doing with that child?"

"Oh, just a pony thing."

Little Ruth hugged Papa around the neck again.

"We know! We'll tell everyone about the greatest Christmas ever, Papa!"

Michael Schall Johnson

A Christmas Treasure

Henry was a young Danish boy, whose father and mother had both died suddenly, leaving to their son only the memory of the happy days of the past. They had presided over the fleeting prosperity and protective love that had been taking care of him over the aura of endless happiness. His father was a merchant and was supposed to be wealthy, but after all his debts were paid Henry Jacobs found himself alone in the world and very destitute.

One evening as he walked out through the suburbs of the city foraging for something to eat, he met a merchant, Hans Gerber, who had been a friend of his father. The old gentleman stopped the boy, and kindly inquired what he was doing and how he had been getting along since his father's death. Henry Jacob had been very dismal and with this man's interest, the tears began to flow down his cheeks till, unable to restrain himself. He embraced his face with his hands and sobbed as if his heart might break.

The old man gave him time to recover and when the boy dashed the tears away with the back of his hand, trying to ease his heartache, said: "I will help you, you are the son of my friend in my youth, I would like to care for you."

He took young Henry by the hand, led him to his own house and provided him with the best of the city. At the age of sixteen, Henry Jacob had grown into a handsome and intelligent young man He started to take great notice of Hans' daughter, the gentle Greta, a fair maiden with beautiful blue eyes, tiny feet and long flowing, blond hair.

One day his benefactor came to him and told him of the distant gold rush in California. He said, "go seek your fortune. I will provide you with everything necessary for the journey, but you must keep a strict budget and before the end of five years send for me and Greta. If you do well, I will reward you doubly, for I love you as if you were my own son."

Hans embraced him tenderly, the eyes of Henry were teared with thankfulness. A gallant ship would soon leave the harbor of Copenhagen, go around the horn and on to the port of San Francisco bound for the gold rush. Hans had given him good advice, which he was thankful for. Just as the ship was about to set sail, the merchant gave to Henry Jacob presented a big black dog, Duke, saying, "This dog has a gift, he will help you to find treasures. Remember everything I have said, beware of robbers and cheats." Again Henry promised, and they embraced, he thought the dog was so old he might not make it to California.

At last, after the usual amount of winds and calms, storms and fair weather, the good ship sailed through the beautiful Golden Gate strait and into the harbor of San Francisco, packed with all manner of ships.

"How happy and rich we shall become in this Golden land," said one man. Henry Jacobs disembarked with his dog, Duke and the other passengers, in a curious land of strangers, where even the language of this country was the patter of an unknown tongue. Fortunately for him, he was not the only Dane in the country, though they were few in number. The Queen city of the Pacific, was a city of many sand hills and a few poor shanties, but it was full of energy, resolve and hope.

Henry Jacobs was a quick, active lad and soon learned enough English to procure a job and for some time remained in San Francisco. He liked the security of the city and wasn't anxious to look for gold. At night, when his work was over, he would take a look at Duke when he saw his dog eager to go. Then the dog started getting a little out of hand and and one day with a growl, he jumped quickly and startled Henry. "One would think you are mad," he said. Then he opened the the door to look out at the bay, hopefully to see a ship coming in. The dog ran out the door and onto the wet streets and was gone all day.

When Duke came back Henry decided it was time to go prospecting, he followed his dog as he seemed eager to lead the way. They at last got to the mountain country, awaking all his wild and eager dreams that he had in the leisure hours of their sea-voyage. At last he found a party of Danish prospectors heading for the mining grounds.

For months Henry Jacobs wandered over the mountains with his comrades, till his shoes were worn out and his trousers and blue shirt so patched with flour-sacks, that it was impossible to distinguish the original material. Still he found nothing, even his comrades lost their eagerness and went back to the city.

One night he sat feeling very sad and wishing he had never left Denmark. A homesick longing to see his native land and his friend and it depressed him. The thought of the kind old man, who had been like a father, troubled him. In his heart he treasured the memory of the merchant's daughter. The gentle Greta maiden with blue eyes and her flowing blond hair.

Just as he was yielding himself to tender dreams of going home, Duke rested his nose on his lap and there he felt a dog's secret. Rising up hastily, he resolved to go off with Duke guiding him and yield to the impulse of the dog. Hoping he might be more successful than in the weary months he had passed with his companions.

With this resolve, the pressure of the to succeed became greater, awaking slumbering hope.

"Where the dog leads me, I will go on to fortune or death; any thing is better than the weariness of my present life."

It was a beautiful, balmy night. The silvery moonlight and the stars brightened even the dim cavern, and flooded the mountains with a luminous beauty. Henry Jacobs went silently up the mountain path until he came to a ledge he had been prospecting early that day. Still Duke urged him on, till he had gone miles farther into the mountains than ever before. About twelve o'clock, he began to get hungry and weary, as it was early evening when he started and after his hard day's work.

Suddenly he could have swore he heard Duke talk, "That is gold," he said. and sat down and as he looked at the ground. Henry looked a the ground, astonished, he saw what appeared to be gold.

Henry looked at this dog to stunned to speak.

"I am my own dog" Duke went on, "and that is satisfying, yet one likes to be cared for and nobody cares for me like you.

"How is it you can talk?" said Hans

"Duke of Ulrich's ancestors were favored by the Oracle of Delphi many centuries ago and a talking dog was his ancestors reward. I am in that lineage of those dogs. Not all of us in the line can speak of course, but I can."

Henry thought he even saw a little smirk on the dogs face. "You also have other significant qualities obviously."

"Hans told me not to just make it easy for you. I talk in a dog language that only you can understand, but I'm very learned and understand all you say. I am an intelligent dog and have many good thoughts."

He looked down at the ground and as he cleared the dirt away a huge stone appeared. He perceived it as the entrance of a huge cavern in the ground, but a big rock was rolled against it. He saw a small opening in which the stone left room for a pry bar. He moved it and through the gap which he barely could see in. He threw himself down on the ground, quite overcome fatigue and taking a piece of hard bread from his pocket, began eating, and thinking of his futile effort.

He was aroused by a harsh voice and looking up, saw, just before him, the immense form of a Grizzly Bear.

"What are you doing here in my country little boy?" said the Grizzly, opening his huge mouth and glaring with his small eyes upon the startled young man.

"He is with me!" spoke up Duke. "

"Thank God, you have saved him, normally the bodies of all who disturb me are carried back in death in caskets to their homeland," said the Grizzly.

"Do you mean to kill me, Mr Grizzly," cried Henry, he could have killed Henry Jacobs with one blow of his giant paw.

"Come here, boy," he said, "I will not hurt you, silly fool not as long as you were brought by Duke, he is one of those special dogs."

Henry Jacobs drew cautiously near the Bear.

"Sit down, and tell me of your wanderings," said the Grizzly, with a rough voice, into which he tried to throw the semblance of kindness.

Henry Jacobs told him all.

"Never mind, boy," said the Grizzly, "you shall win the prize, and go back to Denmark a rich man. See, the morning sun is rising. Now we will enter the cavern and you shall have as much gold as you can carry away."

Henry Jacobs felt a momentary thrill of joy in his heart, which was saddened by the memory of Hans' last words, "Beware of the robbers." He felt kind of like a robber.

Henry thought 'I have wandered in this cold, strange land, and found nothing until now. Wealth is within my grasp; if I do not seize it, I may never have another chance. I will take the risk.' Then he spoke aloud, in a resolute voice, "Lead on, I will follow." Then he Henry turned to Duke and said, "How can you talk to him?"

"I can talk to any animal or human. I have a special status with animals, they all know who I am when I talk to them."

The Grizzly gave the giant stone a push with his great paw and rolled it away as though it was a pebble. As they entered he struck a torch, then, before proceeding, rolled back the stone and closed up the opening. When Henry Jacobs saw himself and Duke shut into the cave with the Grizzly, he trembled with fear, for he saw there was no way of escape. He felt now, he had only to follow wherever the bear might lead them. They went through a long, narrow passage, then down many steps, until at last they entered big cavern. Henry was almost blinded by the reflection of the great masses of gold which lay scattered about and huge seams ran through the rugged sides of the cavern.

"Is this rich enough for you?" said the Grizzly, laughingly. "Help yourself, lad, you remember I told you, you can have all you can carry away."

The delighted Henry Jacobs began to gather up the gold into his sack and a double sack to for Duke carrying on his back. When he had secured all he could pack, he threw the sack over his shoulder, he thanked the Grizzly and begged him to let him go.

"Go on!" replied the Grizzly, with a mocking laugh. "You're welcome to the treasure, but I'm thinking you'll find it hard work to move that stone from the mouth of the cave."

Then Henry threw down the treasure at his feet, crying, with tears in his eyes, "Take back your riches, and let me go out into the sunshine! the beautiful sunshine! Oh! good Grizzly, take back your gold, and give me and my dog liberty!"

"What a fool! go on! go on!" said the Grizzly, and then he laughed as the boulder rolled away with one mighty swat from the bear's paw. Henry and Duke took their sacks of gold and quickly fled. They heard the great stone roll back, striking the opening with such force that the whole mountain shook, and the mighty echo reverberated from all the neighboring mountains.

The longing to send to Denmark for Hans and Greta was ever growing in his heart. He thought sadly of the man who welcomed him into his heart and the he sighed as he dreamed of Greta.

They started quickly for the city worried about the robbers he was warned about, so they started at dusk, planning to travel at night with Duke for his guide.

He was young, healthy and acclimatized to the hardships of a mountain life. For hours they walked on as Duke guided him, until near morning, when they were overcome with fatigue. He threw himself upon the ground among the thick sage brush, and soon fell asleep. A golden fading of the light fell upon him, he rose full of bright hopes, they ate their scanty breakfast and started upon their way with happy hearts.Thus they wandered on for several days, careful of every ledge that they came upon.

Their stock of food was nearly exhausted. Duke and his hopeful nature drove them on, but Henry's dread of a lonely death in the mountains kept him going. One night he struck a fire in a lonely place, and sat down to eat his supper, just as the twilight gave place to the stars of night.He was getting quite disheartened. "I must start for the camp," he said to himself.

Duke was eager to travel that evening and and said to his master, "I smell gold, let's go!"

Duke led them to a ravine that was teeming with another gold find. "Wow, you did it again what are we going to do with all this gold? I'm rich beyond all of my dreams!"

"Don't forget who found it."

"Don't worry you will have a pampered life!"

He fell into all sort of musings and dreams as he drifted off to sleep that night, from which he was aroused by the soft voice of his old Danish companion Fritz who stood before him. His face was wrinkled and sad-looking, yet there was a hopefulness in his expression, Henry's heart warmed as he pleasantly asked, "Why so sorrowful tonight, my boy?"

"I am very happy to see you, let me tell you." All his old companions gathered around him. Then he told them the whole story. "I have not forgotten my old friends we will share equally all the gold we have found."

The happy miners all shook hands with Henry Jacobs. "God bless you, boy." The tears glistened in their eyes, and they thought of their dear ones in distant lands.

That night they all dreamed golden dreams, full of love and happiness.

In the morning they all went together to the newly discovered treasure, which proved to be a large tract of the very rich diggings.

In six months they were all rich beyond all their wildest dreams, and left the mountains for San Fransisco. Five of his six comrades, including Henry sent for their families to come to California and Fritz went back to Denmark.

When at last the ship arrived, and there were new faces looking eagerly about for all the old familiar ones, and the old were looking for the new. So there was altogether a great bustle such has never seen, only in those days when the ships came in from the old country. Henry's friend and benefactor Hans embraced him tenderly, the eyes of Henry were moistened with tears of happiness. He looked forward eagerly to the embrace with Greta, who was even more beautiful than he had remembered.

Hans petted Duke, saying, "This dog gets a gift." He handed him a meaty bone and had a delicious smell that was quite appealing to Duke. It was so pleasant to see the dog eat, that Henry could not leave him until he had finished.

"I enjoyed it greatly." Duke told Henry how good it was in dog language. He was a special dog, and Henry thought how much he owed this animal.

The old Danes got together to talk about the land that was offered for sale , 300 miles to the south. They were unanimous in the idea to get enough land to make a new Danish community in this paradise, with its ideal weather.

Most of the recent arrivals from Denmark traveled with Henry and Hans to the Rancho San Carlos de Jonata by steamer To Port Avila and then coach to the Rancho. This land was part of a Mexican land granted by Pio Pico in the Santa Ynez River Valley part of Santa Barbara County. They eagerly made a deal with the broker. Then they met with a lawyer when they got back to San Francisco and formed a corporation and made Henry the President.

Thus the day passed and they moved to their new land and settled in the old ranch house and the old out buildings. The evening came on, it was raining bleakly, it was Christmas eve.There sat the great dog with his shaggy coat to keep him warm.

After all this great fortune in the new land, Henry was able to give his friend Hans, much more money than he had advanced him. Hans was so happy and after all it was Christmas Eve and they had a big fiesta . So Hans thought and thought, he noticed the love in Henry's eyes whenever he set eyes on his beautiful daughter. He thought of the the greatest gift he could give Henry. So tonight he rewarded him with the hand of his daughter, the beautiful Greta much to the delight of everyone. In all California could not be found a happier man than Henry Jacobs. Tomorrow will be Christmas! He wondered, if anyone will remember this of all as I do, my greatest day ever.!"

The End

Made in the USA
Middletown, DE
04 September 2020